My MAGIC family

Lotte Jeffs
& Sharon Davey

PUFFIN

For Jenny and Ettie, my magic family – L.J.

To Neve and Alex, always – S.D.

PUFFIN BOOKS

UK | USA | Canada | Ireland | Australia | India | New Zealand | South Africa

Puffin Books is part of the Penguin Random House group of companies
whose addresses can be found at global.penguinrandomhouse.com.

www.penguin.co.uk   www.puffin.co.uk   www.ladybird.co.uk

Penguin
Random House
UK

First published 2022

001

Text copyright © Lotte Jeffs, 2022
Illustrations copyright © Sharon Davey, 2022

The moral right of the author and illustrator has been asserted

Printed and bound in China

The authorized representative in the EEA is Penguin Random House Ireland, Morrison Chambers, 32 Nassau Street, Dublin D02 YH68

A CIP catalogue record for this book is available from the British Library

ISBN: 978–0–241–54013–8

All correspondence to:
Puffin Books, Penguin Random House Children's, One Embassy Gardens, 8 Viaduct Gardens, London SW11 7BW

There are *billions* of families,
a *million* ways to be . . .

and in my magic family it's
Mama,
Mum
and me.

Mum makes my breakfast – porridge, toast and jam.

Abracadabra! Whizzo! Wow! Kabam!

Mama blows me kisses, and waves. "I love you, bye!
I'm late for work – it's time to go.
I REALLY have to fly!"

I wonder whether all the **children** have two mums like me.
At nursery school our teacher says, "Why don't we ask and see!

Let's tell our **home-life** stories – fantastical and true –
and we'll find out who's who to me,
and who is who to you."

Gia puts her hand up. "Can I go first?" she cries.
She spins in **sparkly** circles and . . .

we can't **believe** our eyes.

"My **daddy** flies a spaceship,
my **mama** comes from Mars.
We built a home to call our own,
up among the **stars**.

At first when we came down to Earth,
I felt a little wary –
until I met my brilliant friend,
a **kind** and **funny** fairy."

Kai is busy drawing, with colours **wild** and **free**.
His pictures seem to come to life for everyone to see.

"My **granny** is a hero,
but she doesn't jump or run.
She likes to take it slightly slow –
and have a nap for fun.

I sometimes have to find her specs –
they often go astray.

But if there's ever **trouble**,
she is there to **save** the day."

Next, we all sit down to sing
"Row, row, row your boat".

Then **Ravi** tells his story . . .

and

we

all

begin

to

float!

"My **daddy** is a pirate,
my **stepmum** rules the sea.
They brave the waves together
and bring pizzas home for tea.

Even when they're busy – finding treasure, reading maps –

they still make time for **snuggles** as I curl up in their laps".

At lunch, **Naomi** conjures up delicious mini cakes.
It's always fun to see the **magic** things her family makes.

"My **daddy** is a wizard
and my **dad** is one as well.
At home we have an ancient book with **every** kind of spell!

They take me on **adventures** and their magic can grant wishes.

They make my **dreams** come true.
(But we still have to wash the dishes!) "

Outside in the garden, we plant
seeds deep in the ground.
Then **Arlo** tells his story as
the bugs and bees buzz round . . .

"My **mum** lives in a giant shoe,
my **dad** lives in the other.
I get to stay with both of them,
and so do all my brothers.

MUM'S SHOE